12 REASONS TO LOVE THE
SAN FRANCISCO GIANTS

by Doug Williams

Walla Walla
County Libraries

www.12StoryLibrary.com

Copyright © 2016 by Peterson Publishing Company, North Mankato, MN 56003. All rights reserved. No part of this book may be reproduced or utilized in any form or by any means without written permission from the publisher.

12-Story Library is an imprint of Peterson Publishing Company and Press Room Editions.

Produced for 12-Story Library by Red Line Editorial

ISBN
978-1-63235-216-3 (hardcover)
978-1-63235-243-9 (paperback)
978-1-62143-268-5 (hosted ebook)

Library of Congress Control Number: 2015934321

Printed in the United States of America
Mankato, MN
October, 2015

Go beyond the book. Get free, up-to-date content on this topic at 12StoryLibrary.com.

TABLE OF CONTENTS

THE GIANTS STAND TALL

From their earliest days, the Giants have been among the best teams in the National League (NL). Their 23 league championships rank number one. Only three teams have won more than the Giants' eight World Series championships.

The Giants' history spans three centuries and two coasts. The team's first season was in 1883 in New York. The team was known as the Gothams. It didn't become known as the Giants until 1885. The Giants won their first NL titles in 1888 and 1889. They won five World Series in New York. Their last was in 1954. The team moved to California after the 1957 season.

As the San Francisco Giants, the team was often blessed with wonderful players. But for the team's first 52 years in California, the Giants didn't win a World Series.

It wasn't until 2010 that the Giants finally won it all. A crazy cast of characters led the way. Long-haired ace pitcher Tim Lincecum, bearded reliever Brian Wilson, and colorful first baseman Aubrey Huff led the Giants past the Texas Rangers in five games. Then they won it again in 2012 and 2014.

3

Complete-game shutouts Christy Mathewson pitched in the 1905 World Series.

- The Giants beat the Philadelphia Athletics for the title.
- The World Series win was the Giants' first.
- The Giants had refused to play the 1904 World Series because manager John McGraw said the upstart American League (AL) was inferior.

Pitcher Madison Bumgarner lifts the World Series trophy after the Giants won their eighth championship in 2014.

WILLIE MAYS DOES IT ALL

A few players hit more home runs than Willie Mays. Others had higher batting averages, stole more bases, and had more hits. But many baseball experts believe Mays was the best all-around player who ever lived.

"If there were a baseball god, it would be him," said former NL president and longtime player Bill White. "Nobody could play like he could. Nobody."

Mays played 21 seasons with the Giants, first in New York and then in San Francisco. He last played for the Giants in 1972. He's still a large presence at AT&T Park in San Francisco. A 9-foot (2.7-m) bronze statue of Willie Howard Mays Jr. stands outside the park's Mays Gate. He's shown gazing into the distance after a swing, as if watching one of his 660 home runs.

When Mays played baseball, his joy was apparent. He was a gifted player who could do it all. Great all-around

Willie Mays was elected to the hall of fame in 1979.

Willie Mays leaps high into the air to make a catch for the Giants in a 1959 game against the Milwaukee Braves.

players in the sport are called five-tool players. They can hit for average, hit with power, run, throw, and field. Mays had all the tools.

"I've answered the question a million times," said legendary Dodgers broadcaster Vin Scully. "'Who's the best player you ever saw?' Hands down, it's Willie."

Mays hit .302 for his career, had 3,283 hits, and led the NL in homers four times. He was elected to the Baseball Hall of Fame in 1979.

THINK ABOUT IT

Who do you believe is the greatest baseball player? What makes him better than the rest? Write three or four sentences to explain your answer.

13

At-bats needed for Willie Mays to record his first major league hit in 1951.

- Mays signed his first professional contract at age 16 in the Negro American League.
- Black players had to play in the Negro Leagues because MLB teams refused to sign black players until 1947.
- He lost almost two full seasons because of military service in 1952 and 1953.
- His 660 home runs were second all-time when he retired in 1973.

THOMSON HITS THE SHOT HEARD 'ROUND THE WORLD

"The Giants win the pennant!" That was the call of New York Giants broadcaster Russ Hodges on October 3, 1951. The call came at the end of perhaps the Giants' best-known game.

The Giants and Brooklyn Dodgers ended the 1951 season tied for first. That set up a best-of-three playoff series. The teams split the first two games. Game 3 was at the Giants' ballpark, the Polo Grounds.

Giants players surround Bobby Thomson after his walk-off home run against the Brooklyn Dodgers in 1951.

The Dodgers scored three runs in the top of the eighth inning. Going to the bottom of the ninth, they led 4–1.

The first two Giants hitters singled. After the third batter fouled out, a double by the fourth hitter scored a run. Then Bobby Thomson came to the plate. Two runners were on base. There was one out. On the second pitch from relief pitcher Ralph Branca, Thomson hit a three-run home run.

Thomson leaped and waved his arms in excitement as he rounded the bases. When he arrived at home plate, he was mobbed by teammates. Joyous fans ran onto the field.

13½

Games by which the Giants trailed the first-place Dodgers in August of 1951.

- The Giants went 37–7 the rest of the way and tied for first on the last day of the season.
- A best-of-three playoff decided the NL pennant.
- Bobby Thomson and Ralph Branca became great friends.

"I can remember feeling as if time was just frozen," Thomson said of the home run. "It was a delirious, delicious moment." The home run is known as "The Shot Heard 'Round the World."

THE MOMENT ON RADIO

Russ Hodges's famous call: "There's a long drive. It's going to be, I believe. . . . The Giants win the pennant! The Giants win the pennant! The Giants win the pennant! The Giants win the pennant! Bobby Thomson hits into the lower deck of the left-field stands! The Giants win the pennant, and they're going crazy! They're going crazy! I don't believe it! I don't believe it! I do not believe it!"

9

BASEBALL'S LONGEST RIVALRY GOES COAST TO COAST

For decades in New York, the Giants had a special rivalry with the Brooklyn Dodgers. They played in the same city. Their ballparks were just a few miles apart. Since 1890, they were both members of the NL. Often the NL championship came down to the Giants and Dodgers. The rivalry was intense. Pitchers from both teams often tried to hit the other team's batters. Fights sometimes broke out in the stands and on the field.

After the 1957 season, both teams moved west. They became the San Francisco Giants and Los Angeles Dodgers. They brought their rivalry with them. Some have called it the best rivalry in sports.

Often the rivalry has involved close pennant races. In 1962 the teams tied for first. The Giants won the best-of-three playoff series to go to the World Series. Three years later, the Giants were up by four games with 12 to play. But San Francisco collapsed. The Dodgers went 11–1 to take the pennant. Said former Dodgers player, coach, and manager

8

US states that are younger than the Giants–Dodgers rivalry.

- The teams first played each other in 1890.
- Brooklyn's team nickname in 1890 was the Bridegrooms.
- The teams twice faced each other in playoffs for the pennant, in 1951 and 1962.

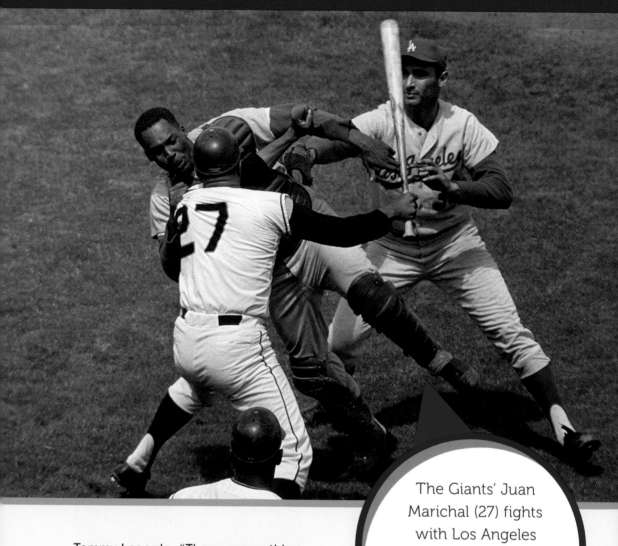

The Giants' Juan Marichal (27) fights with Los Angeles Dodgers catcher John Roseboro and pitcher Sandy Koufax during a 1965 game.

Tommy Lasorda, "There was nothing better than beating the Giants."

Sometimes the rivalry has been violent. In 1965, Giants pitcher Juan Marichal attacked Dodgers catcher John Roseboro with a bat. Before a game in 1973, Lasorda brought the lineup card to home plate and got into a fight with Giants manager Charlie Fox. Said former Dodgers shortstop Maury Wills, "Anything can happen when the Dodgers and Giants are playing."

5

THE GIANTS SHINE IN THE BALLPARK BY THE BAY

There are many wonderful ballparks, but perhaps the most scenic is AT&T Park in San Francisco. Opened in 2000, the park sits alongside San Francisco Bay. Seagulls circle overhead during games. Meanwhile, the smell of the bay mixes with aromas from the concession stands where garlic fries and clam chowder are sold.

Fans can look out to right field and see ships. They can look beyond left field at the Bay Bridge. Around the stadium, fans can find an old cable car and statues of Giants legends. What most people remember, however, is McCovey Cove. Long home runs to right field land in the cove. Fans often wait in their

boats to collect the balls. Inside the stadium, a sign in right field keeps count of the Giants' "splash hits."

355 feet (108 m)

Distance from home plate to McCovey Cove down the right-field line.

- The cove is named after former Giants first baseman Willie McCovey.
- The depth of cove is 20–28 feet (6–8.5 m), depending on the tides.
- The average water temperature is 58 degrees Fahrenheit (14°C).
- Giants slugger Barry Bonds had 35 "splash hits."

COLD, WINDY CANDLESTICK

Before moving to AT&T Park, the Giants had played at Candlestick Park since 1960. That multipurpose stadium was shared with the football 49ers. And it often wasn't a fun place to watch or play a game. It could be foggy, freezing, and windy. "There was nowhere to hide from it," said former Giant J. T. Snow. "You just had to accept it." The Giants' new home was built specifically for baseball.

AT&T Park in San Francisco

BOCHY PROVES TO BE THE RIGHT MAN FOR THE JOB

Bruce Bochy places the Giants' 2012 World Series trophy on display before a game the next season.

.494

Bruce Bochy's winning percentage in 12 seasons before coming to the Giants.

- He had a .515 winning percentage in his first eight seasons with the Giants.
- His postseason winning percentage from 2010 to 2014 was .708.

THINK ABOUT IT

How much difference does a manager make? How can he help win more games? How can he hurt the team? Write three or four sentences to explain your answer.

In October of 2006, the Giants were in a slump. The team hadn't been to the playoffs since 2003. It had just completed its worst two seasons in 10 years. San Francisco wanted a new manager to turn things around. Enter Bruce Bochy.

The former San Diego Padres manager was looking for a change. The Giants were looking for a change maker. When Bochy signed with the team, he said he hoped to make "an impact and a contribution." Did he ever. Bochy led the Giants to World Series titles in 2010, 2012, and 2014. They were the first three championships for the team since moving to San Francisco in 1958.

Bochy built teams with strong pitching staffs and managed them well. He gave young players the chance to grow. He also got the most out of older players. His success with the Giants may take him to the Baseball Hall of Fame. Every manager with at least three World Series titles has been elected.

"If your leader is a rock as solid as Bochy is, if your leader is as sharp as Bochy is, it leaks into the team," said Giants outfielder Hunter Pence. "We believe in him."

BUSTER BUSTS OUT

Early in 2010, the Giants were having trouble scoring runs. So they called up their top minor league prospect, catcher Buster Posey. In his first game that season, the 23-year-old Posey had three hits and drove in three runs. And the Giants won.

Both trends continued. Posey ended the year as the NL Rookie of the Year. The Giants ended the year as World Series champions.

"What Buster did handling the pitching staff, handling himself, and

Buster Posey tags out the Philadelphia Phillies' Carlos Ruiz at home during a 2010 playoff game.

NO SPEED? NO PROBLEM

In his first year at Florida State University, Buster Posey was a good shortstop. But his coaches weren't convinced. They saw his leadership ability, toughness, strong arm, and below-average speed. Those skills, they believed, meant he would be a perfect catcher. So he switched. As a junior in 2008, he was college baseball's player of the year and the fifth overall draft pick by the Giants.

hitting in the heart of the order shows you what a tremendous kid he is," manager Bruce Bochy said.

Two years later, Posey hit .336 to win the NL batting title. He was also named NL Most Valuable Player (MVP). The Giants won the World Series again that year, and Posey was also a key player when they won again two years later.

Buster Posey developed into one of the NL's most dangerous hitters.

.336

Buster Posey's league-leading batting average in 2012.

- He became the first NL catcher since 1942 to win a batting title.
- Posey hit 24 home runs and drove in 103 runs.

FANS SING SONGS TO BELIEVE IN

The Giants have a late-game tradition. Since 2010, the team has played one of two songs before the bottom of the eighth inning. Both are 1980s hits from the Bay Area rock group Journey.

If the Giants are ahead, "Lights" is played. If the game is tied or the Giants are trailing, "Don't Stop Believin'" comes on. Either way, fans at AT&T Park get up to sing.

Steve Perry, the former lead singer of Journey and a lifelong Giants fan, often comes to AT&T Park for big games to lead the sing-along.

Giants fans never stopped believin' in 2014. The team played the St. Louis Cardinals in the 2014

NL Championship Series (NLCS). In the deciding game, "Don't Stop Believin'" played. Moments later, pinch hitter Michael Morse hit a game-tying home run. The Giants went on to win in the ninth.

2010

Year the Giants began playing "Don't Stop Believin'" or "Lights" in the eighth inning.

- Journey released "Don't Stop Believin'" in 1981.
- The Chicago White Sox also used the song during their run to the 2005 World Series championship.
- Former Journey lead singer Steve Perry grew up a Giants fan and wanted the songs associated with his team.

Former Journey lead signer Steve Perry leads Giants fans in "Don't Stop Believin'" before a 2014 playoff game at AT&T Park.

"Don't Stop Believin'" has also been played after big wins and World Series victory parades. Today when the song comes on in San Francisco, many people think of the Giants.

THE LEFTY IS LIGHTS OUT

Madison Bumgarner thrives under pressure. He showed that as a 21-year-old rookie in 2010. That September, the 6-foot-5 lefty from North Carolina won two games as the Giants won the division by two. His earned-run average (ERA) for the month was just 1.13.

In the playoffs, his 3–2 win over the Atlanta Braves clinched a spot in the NLCS. Bumgarner showed poise under playoff pressure that manager Bruce Bochy said was "beyond his years." Then in the World Series against the Texas Rangers, "Mad Bum" won again to help the Giants to a championship.

Bumgarner won 60 games over the next four seasons as the Giants won two more World Series. Bay Area fans came to love the quiet, hard-throwing country boy.

Madison Bumgarner pitches against the Texas Rangers in the 2010 World Series.

Giants catcher Buster Posey lifts Madison Bumgarner into the air in celebration after the team's 2014 World Series win.

In the 2014 postseason, he won four games, including two in the World Series. He also came out of the bullpen to save Game 7. Said Giants reliever Jeremy Affeldt after Game 7, "It was the greatest pitching performance that I've ever seen. The whole World Series. What he did, I'm speechless. . . . He was so calm and focused."

1.03

Madison Bumgarner's ERA in seven postseason games in 2014.

- He was MVP of the 2014 World Series and NLCS.
- He had four wins, one save, and one loss in the 2014 postseason.
- Bumgarner went 7–3 with a 2.14 ERA in the 2010, 2012, and 2014 postseasons.

21

THE GREATEST GIANTS STAND TALLER THAN THE REST

In his 22 years with the New York Giants, outfielder Mel Ott was the NL's most feared slugger. He led the league in home runs six times and was the first in the NL to hit 500 homers. When he retired in 1947, he held almost every Giants hitting record. Ott is one of 11 Giants honored in a display at AT&T Park. It's a link to the team's long history.

Four of those honored are pitchers. They are Carl Hubbell, Juan Marichal, Christy Mathewson, and Gaylord Perry. First basemen Bill Terry, Orlando Cepeda, and Willie McCovey are also honored. So are outfielders Monte Irvin and Willie Mays. John McGraw is the only manager on the list. Microphones represent team announcers Lon Simmons,

The New York Giants' Mel Ott was one of the team's best hitters of all time.

12

Years after Monte Irvin signed his first pro contract in the Negro Leagues before he was allowed to play in the major leagues.

- Irvin debuted for the Giants at age 30 in 1949.
- In his second full season, he hit .312 with a league-leading 121 runs batted in.
- He was elected into the Baseball Hall of Fame in 1973.

Russ Hodges, and Jon Miller. In addition, all MLB teams honor Jackie Robinson, baseball's first black player.

All the players and McGraw are in the Baseball Hall of Fame. In total, 29 players who spent large parts of their careers with the Giants are in the hall.

JUST DANDY

Giants pitcher Juan Marichal was called "The Dominican Dandy." He had a windup like no other. The star of the 1960s and 1970s kicked his left leg almost shoulder high as he balanced on his right leg before the pitch. He won 243 games overall and was a nine-time All-Star.

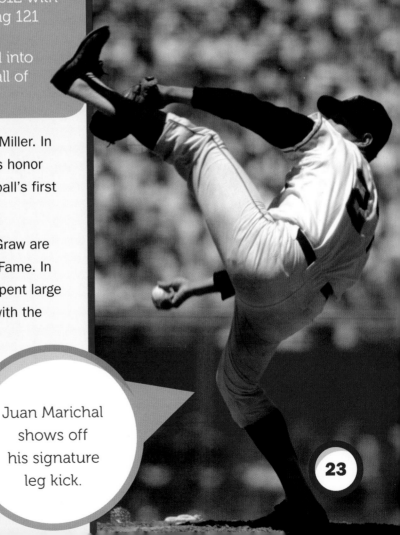

Juan Marichal shows off his signature leg kick.

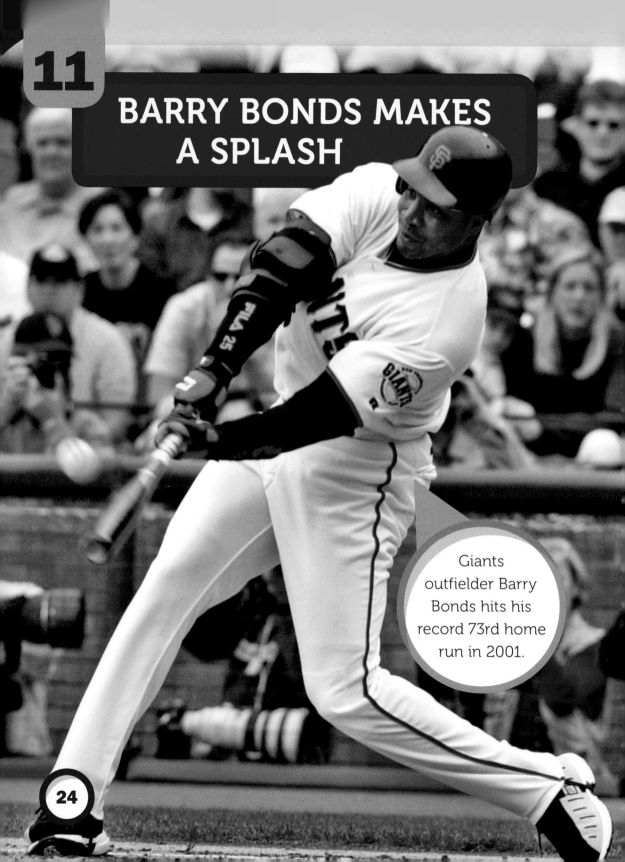

BARRY BONDS MAKES A SPLASH

Giants outfielder Barry Bonds hits his record 73rd home run in 2001.

The Giants' record book reads like a who's who of baseball history. It features names like Willie Mays, Christy Mathewson, and Mel Ott. Perhaps the most dominant Giant, however, was Barry Bonds. With the Giants, he hit a record 73 homers in 2001. He also broke baseball's career home run record in 2007. His 756th passed Hank Aaron. From 2001 to 2004, he was the NL's MVP. He also is the team's all-time leader in on-base percentage, slugging percentage, and walks.

Though Bonds' numbers are worthy of the hall of fame, he has not been elected. Many voters have refused to vote for him because he's been accused of using performance-enhancing drugs. In San Francisco, however, he is still cheered.

Mays still leads the Giants with 2,857 games played, 3,187 hits, and 646 home runs. Pitcher Mathewson won a team-record 372 games with a 2.12 ERA and 2,504 strikeouts. Ott drove in 1,860 runs. More recently, closer Brian Wilson tied Rod Beck with 48 saves in one season.

.401

Batting average of first baseman Bill Terry in 1930, the only Giants player to hit .400.

- Terry shares the NL record for hits in a season with 254 in 1930.
- He was elected to the Baseball Hall of Fame in 1954.
- Terry served as both player and manager for the Giants for five seasons.

THINK ABOUT IT

Would you vote Barry Bonds into the hall of fame? How should MLB deal with players suspected of using performance-enhancing drugs? Write three or four sentences to explain your answers.

LUIGI GIVES THE GIANTS A SEAL OF APPROVAL

Officially, his name is quite formal: Luigi Francisco Seal. But around AT&T Park where he lives and works, he's known as Lou Seal. The costumed character is the Giants' mascot.

Lou Seal is a big presence at every Giants home game and a fan favorite. He takes part in pregame ceremonies. He also rides around on a scooter. He dances on top of the dugouts between innings and roams through the stands, hugging and high-fiving fans. When the Giants had their victory parade through San Francisco after winning the 2014 World Series, Lou Seal was in the lead vehicle, holding up a championship belt.

Lou Seal has been around since 1999. Through 2014, the same person had worn the costume since Lou Seal's first appearance and had never missed a home game.

25

Weight, in pounds (11 kg), of the head of the Lou Seal costume.

- The costume is hot inside. The person who wears it loses 6–8 pounds (2.7–3.6 kg) each game.
- Lou Seal wears an extra-large World Series ring.
- Lou Seal makes 250 public appearances each year.

THINK ABOUT IT

Do mascots help you enjoy watching a baseball game? How do they affect your game-day experience, positively or negatively?

CRAZY CRAB

In 1984, the Giants had a mascot called Crazy Crab. He was meant as a sort of joke at a time when other teams were coming up with new mascots. He was a big, orange, foam-rubber crab with large, crazy eyes. But during a 96-loss season, fans often yelled at him and pelted him with thrown objects. He lasted just one season.

Lou Seal dresses up for Star Wars Day at AT&T Park in 2011.

12 KEY DATES

1883

A new NL team is formed called the New York Gothams. Two years later, manager Jim Mutrie called the team "his giants" after a big win. The nickname stuck.

1904

The Giants qualify for the second World Series but refuse to play. Manager John McGraw didn't believe the new AL was a true competitor to the NL.

1905

The Giants sweep the Philadelphia Athletics to win their first World Series.

1951

The Giants' Bobby Thomson hits a three-run home run in the ninth inning to clinch the pennant over the rival Brooklyn Dodgers.

1954

Willie Mays makes perhaps the greatest catch in World Series history. In Game 1 against the Cleveland Indians, with the score tied and two runners on in the eighth inning, he makes an over-the-shoulder catch of a ball hit 460 feet (140 m) to center field by Vic Wertz.

1957

Team owner Horace Stoneham decides to move the Giants from New York to San Francisco after the season.

1979

Giants' great Willie Mays is elected into the National Baseball Hall of Fame.

2000

The Giants move into what is now AT&T Park. It is considered one of the best ballparks in baseball.

2001

Barry Bonds sets a major league record when he hits 73 home runs.

2010

After more than five decades in San Francisco, the Giants win their first World Series out west.

2012

Giants catcher Buster Posey is named NL MVP and the team wins another World Series.

2014

Madison Bumgarner has four wins, one save, and one loss in the 2014 postseason. He is named World Series MVP after the Giants beat the Kansas City Royals.

GLOSSARY

ace
A team's best starting pitcher.

call
A live description by a radio or TV announcer of the play-by-play of a baseball game.

contract
A legal agreement between a player and a team. Common factors covered in a contract include salary and years of service.

ERA
The average number of earned runs a pitcher gives up per nine innings.

manager
The person in charge of the team during games.

mascot
A character, usually in costume, who represents the team and entertains fans at a game.

pennant
A league championship.

prospect
A young player within an organization who has the potential to be a major leaguer.

retire
To end one's career.

rivalry
A long, competitive relationship between teams.

rookie
A first-year player in a league.

save
When a relief pitcher maintains his team's lead of three or fewer runs while finishing a game.

FOR MORE INFORMATION

Books

Baggarly, Andrew. *A Band of Misfits: Tales of the 2010 San Francisco Giants.* Chicago: Triumph Books, 2011.

Fost, Dan. *The Giants Baseball Experience: A Year-By-Year Chronicle, from New York to San Francisco.* Minneapolis, MN: Quayside Publishing Group, 2014.

Murphy, Brian. *San Francisco Giants: 50 Years.* San Rafael, CA: Insight Editions, 2008.

Websites

Baseball Reference
www.baseball-reference.com

National Baseball Hall of Fame
www.baseballhall.org

San Francisco Giants
www.sanfrancisco.giants.mlb.com

INDEX

About the Author

Doug Williams is a freelance writer in San Diego, California. He is a former newspaper reporter. He's written several books about sports and writes for many national and San Diego-area publications. He is a lifelong baseball fan.